WRITER

ABC

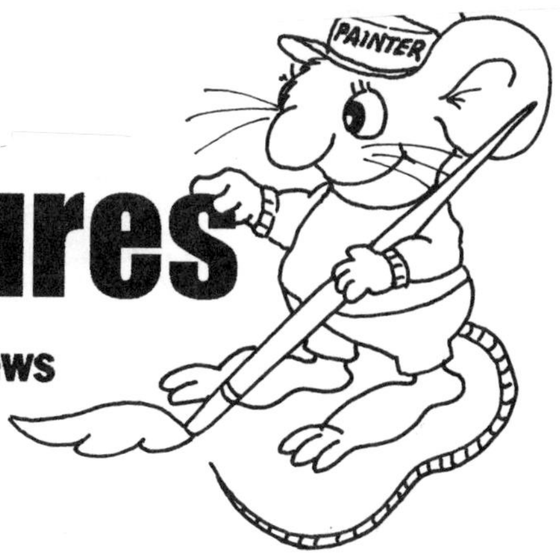

PAINTER

As featured in the Dayton Daily News

Book 3

ABC-What Job Do You See?

Hidden Picture Puzzles

By Liz Ball

What is your job?

HOW MANY CAN YOU FIND?

ARTIST

Over 1300 Hidden Objects!

TEACHER

Hidden Treasures

ABC

SINGER

FUN!

56 Pages of FUN!

Published by Hidden Pictures

Printed in the United States of America

LIZ BALL'S
Hidden Picture
Puzzles
Are you an Artist?
Liz Ball
Hidden Treasures By Liz Ball
© Liz Ball
I like to draw!
Holiday Hidden Treasures
SOCK
MOTH
CROWN
BAND-AID
MUSIC NOTE
ARTIST BRUSH
NEEDLE
SPOON
TOOTHBRUSH
CUPCAKE
TENNIS BALL
ICE CREAM CONE
(5) BIRDS
WORM
(4) HEARTS
MUSHROOM
BELL
(2) CARROTS
EYE GLASSES
SALT SHAKER
CANDLE
A

I'm an Astronaut
SPACE
ASTRO
USA
ASTRO
NASA
©Liz Ball
What is your favorite job?
FLAG
SHOE
WORM
(2) TEPEES
ARROWHEAD
ENVELOPE
HOUSE
SCREW
BRUSH
(2) SOCKS
CANDLE RING
HEART
CONE
BOOMERANG
MEGAPHONE
BANDAID
SLICE OF BREAD
THERMOS
BALL
BOOT
NAIL

BEARY'S BOOKSTORE
NONFICTION
MYSTERY
FANTASY
SALE 25% OFF
ONCE UPON A TIME
BUGS
Hidden Treasures
Hidden Picture Puzzles
by
LIZ BALL
Alphabet Book
B
Read any good books lately?
© Liz Ball
BOOMERANG
(2) MUGS
CROWN
BALL BAT
TOOTHBRUSH
PEPPERMINT
RULER
(2) ENVELOPES
HARMONICA
CRAYON
GOLF CLUB
(3) PENCILS
CHALK
GUM
HOTDOG
TOOTH
FLAG
TEPEE
TOOTHPICK
FLASHLIGHT
NECK TIE
LADDER
SOCK
Do bears read books?

Do you like to bake?
COOKIES
COOKIES
© Liz Ball
This is a "beary" good cookie!
PENCIL
TOOTHPICK
PARTY HAT
CANOE
LADLE
CANDLE
GOOSE
BOOMERANG
FLAG
POPSICLE
BOOT
SALT SHAKER
(2) TEPEES
BELL
(2) HEARTS
FRIED EGG
CANDY
SOCK
SPATULA
HORSE

What a comedian!
BEARY GOOD BEAR JOKES
STICK OF GUM
SALTSHAKER
HOUSE
TIN CUP
LADDER
SAILBOAT
RULER
PENCIL
ENVELOPE
(3) CONES
(2) SOCKS
FLUTE
UMBRELLA
CANOE
SPIDER
TENNIS SHOE
Ha Ha Ha
Heh Heh Heh
C

My e-mail address is HiddenPictures@aol.com

Do you use e-mail?

COMPUTER TIPS EASY AS 1-2-3

CTRL S

INK JET

BUFFALO

POCKET KNIFE

DINOSAUR

PAINT BRUSH

LADDER

ENVELOPE

CROSS

CLOTHES PIN

RULER

WORM

THREAD

DUCK

BOOT

CANOE

SAILBOAT

SLICE OF BREAD

TEPEE

CUPCAKE

CRAYON

NEEDLE

RABBIT

Am I a Computer bug?

Who is your Doctor ?
Certificate from the School of Internal Medicine
Harry Bark MD
Internist
Medicine Book
ANATOMY Vol. 3
COTTON BALLS
ALCOHOL
DOCTOR
©Liz Ball
SYRINGE
SHOE
SPECIMEN JAR
PENCIL
ENVELOPE
THERMOMETER
BAR OF SOAP
SWAB
REFLEX HAMMER
STETHOSCOPE
SOCK
OTOSCOPE
HEART
TONGUE COMPRESSER
JUMP ROPE
RULER
PENNY
(2) BAND-AIDS
MAGNET
EYE DROPPER

Dancing is so romantic!
DANCER
© Liz Ball
Do you want to dance?
GENIE LAMP
(6) HEARTS
HORSE
TOOTHBRUSH
CANOE
SNAKE
MOUTH
TEPEE
(3) BIRDS
SOCK
MUSHROOM
BUTTERFLY
DOG
KEY
GINGERBREAD MAN
CHOCOLATE KISS
CANDY CORN

These frogs are Entertainers!
©Liz Ball
CROWN
(2) SPOONS
BUTTERFLY
IRON
(4)TEPEES
BELL
MUSIC NOTE
CASTANETS
MOUTH
BEETLE
MANDOLIN
HORN
PONY
WATCH
HEART
TROWEL

Do you know what an Editor does?
MOM
THURSDAY
18
A-E
EDITOR
©E.Ball
PENGUIN
RULER
SUN HAT
CANDY-CANE
RABBIT
SAILBOAT
CANOE
WALKIE TALKIE
MUSHROOM
IRON
TOOTH BRUSH
ENVELOPE
BOOT
CROWN
TEPEE
ORANGE SLICE
LADDER
CATERPILLAR
CLOTHES-PIN

F
TO THE BEST DAD
HAPPY FATHER'S DAY
©Liz Ball
LADDER
NECKTIE
SAIL-BOAT
SHOE
TEPEE
CUP
STICK OF GUM
(5) HEARTS
COWBOY BOOT
BASEBALL CAP
FISHING POLE
SOCKS (2)
(2) CARROTS
FOOTBALL
BANANA
ALLIGATOR
HIKING BOOT
CROWN
GOLF CLUB
BIRD
KNIFE
SCREW-DRIVER

I am a Firefly
I think he's a waterbug!
I want to be a Fireman!
5
SPARKY
© Liz Ball
FLASHLIGHT
(2) HEARTS
(2) CROWNS
ORANGE
PEAR
LADDER
STICK OF GUM
BALL
AXE
MEGAPHONE
BELL
PACIFIER
HAND WEIGHT
FLOWER POT
BEE SKEP
PIE
RING
BAT
SHOE
BOOT

© Liz Ball
I do not like Fishermen.
SHOE
ARTIST BRUSH
DOG HEAD
CUP
ICE SKATE
MOUSE
KNIFE
TURTLE
CARROT
CONE
SOCK
ALSO FIND:
(1) BIG BOOT
GOBLET
BOAT
PENCIL
WORM
FUNNEL
JUMP ROPE

I am a Farmer!
©Liz Ball
MAGNET
BRUSH
CUPCAKE
FOOTBALL
BONE
GLOVE
PADLOCK
(2) CONES
BOOMERANG
IRON
CANOE
(2) PENCILS
CUP
HAMBURGER
(2) HEARTS
SKILLET
MOUSE
CROWN
PEPPERMINT

NEXT TEE
I am a gopher, not a golfer!
SLICE OF BREAD
SQUIRREL
NEEDLE
GOLF TEE
CROWN
SHOE
RABBIT
POPSICLE
HIGH TOP BOOT
SLEEPING DRAGON
BIRD
(2) TEPEES
FISH HOOK
CAMP KNIFE
RULER
WORM

Are you a Gardener?
DINOSAUR
MOUSE
SALTSHAKER
TURTLE
(2) SPOONS
BUTTON
(4) CARROTS
LIPS
CROWN
(2) SHOES
PEAR
(2) CONES
ROCKING HORSE
(2) HEARTS
(3) BIRDS
GNAT

Frogella's Hair Salon
Cut
Perms
Style
Hairdos
Are you a Hair Stylist?
©Liz Ball
CURLER
(2) PEARS
DONUT
PENNY
CANDLE
CANDY CORN
WORM
(2) BIRDS
FLUTE
CURLING IRON
PENCIL
HAMBURGER
BANANA
MUSHROOM
COMB
NAIL FILE
SOCK
NAIL BRUSH
(2) TEPEES
HEART
SLIPPER
More Curl Hair Gel

Wow! What a shot!

HOCKEY

© Liz Ball

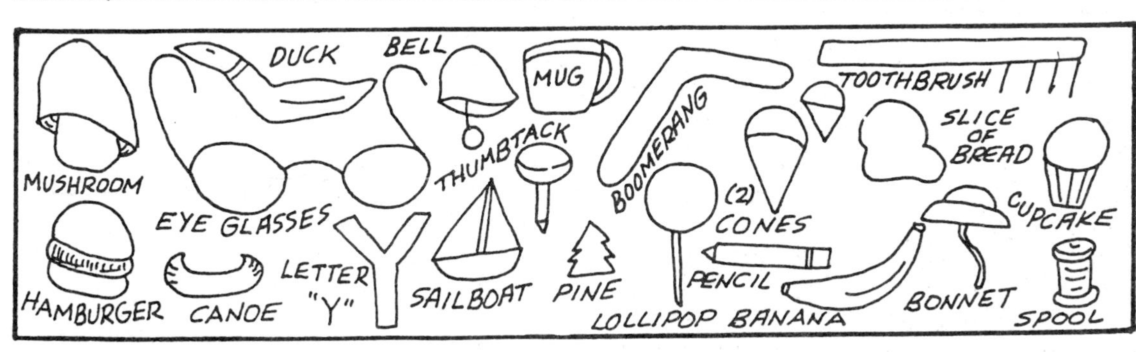

What is your favorite flavor?
IGUANA'S HOMEMADE ICE CREAM
HOORAY FOR ICE CREAM
ROCK SALT
ICE
© Liz Ball
PENCIL
IVY LEAF
YAM
SCREW
INK PEN
LADDER
(2) BIRDS
WISH BONE
CHICK
(2) ICE CREAM CONES
MAILBOX
MITTEN
INSECT
PIE
CANDLE
IRON
SALT SHAKER
TEPEE
IVORY TUSK

Can you ice skate and eat ice cream at the same time?

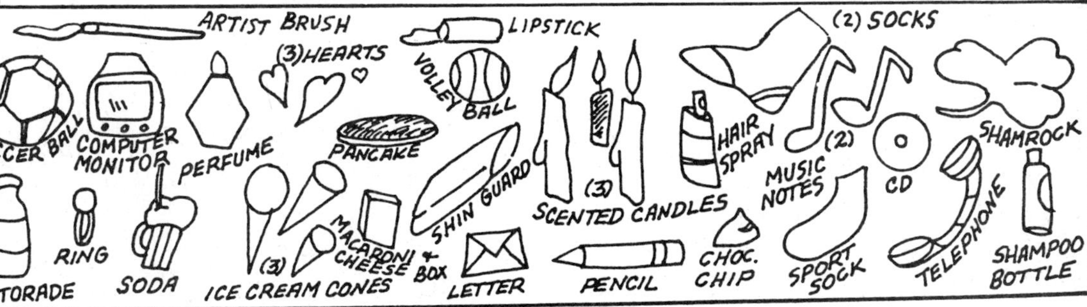

JELLY
JAM
Jelly
JAM
JELLY
JELLY
JAM
JELLY
JAM
JAM
Jelly
JAM
1 CUP
1/2 CUP
1/4 CUP
JAM
FLOUR
SUGAR
COOK BOOK
JAM & JELLY
I like Jam!
© Liz Ball
PEACH JAM
GRAPE JELLY
JAM
PEAR JAM
JELLY
CHERRY
NEEDLE
SHOE
(2) RINGS
TRAFFIC LIGHT
FLAG
CONE
TELESCOPE
BANANA
SALT SHAKER
POPSICLE
BELL
BREAD
RULER
CANDLE
(4) TEPEES
CANOE
SAILBOAT
PENCIL
MATCH
(2) CROWNS

PITCHER
CROWN
CARROT
SHOVEL
SAILBOAT
CANOE
HIGH HEEL
TOOTH-BRUSH
PLANE
HEART
SPOON
CHICK
FISH
STAR
MITTEN
DINOSAUR
ICE CREAM CONE
EYE GLASSES
FROG
LADYBUG
© Liz Ball

Здравствуйте
HALLO
HELLO
Shalom
Bonjour!
H I
DO YOU KNOW SIGN LANGUAGE?
Gutentag
HOLA
こんにちは
KON NICHI WA
ENGLISH TO JAPANESE
LANGUAGE FESTIVAL
© E.C. Ball
I'm a Linguist.
WOODEN SHOE
MITTEN
BIRD
RADIO
TELEPHONE
TURTLE
RABBIT
PENCIL
SPOON
WATCH
LIGHTNING FLASH
CANOE
HEART
TEPEE
PITCHER
STARFISH
BRUSH
RULER
BASEBALL
LADDER

Do you have a library card?
Wormster's Dictionary
W is for WORM
CHARLOTTE'S WEB
SQUIRMY WORMY POEMS
BUTTERFLIES and MOTHS
Hidden Treasures
©Liz Ball
I'm a Librarian.
SAILBOAT
(2) MUGS
(2) CONES
FLASHLIGHT
LETTER
BOOMERANG
SHOE
SCRUB BRUSH
(2) HEARTS
CHERRY
CANDY STICK
SOCK
(2) CANDY CORN
IRON
PENCIL
BLUE JEANS
(2) TEPEES
TUNING FORK
CLOTHES PIN
KNIFE

Music is fun!
Do you play the piano?
M
I'm a Musician.
©Liz Ball
BIRD
(3) MUSIC NOTES
TELESCOPE
MUG
SAILBOAT
BUTTERFLY
WREN
TOOTHBRUSH
CROWN
CRAYON
PAIR OF PANTS
PENCIL
LADDER
FLASHLIGHT
PEAR
HEART
CLOTHESPIN
POCKET KNIFE
BANANA
LADLE
BASEBALL

To: Firefly
I need a stamp.
TWEET
JAY
To: Bobbie Robin
19 Elm Tree Ln.
Dayton, OH 45416
©Liz Ball
My dad was a Mailman!
To: My Friend
FISH
HEART
MATCH
GUM
BONE
SNO CONE
CHERRY
CROWN
WISHBONE
(2) BIRDS
FLAG
HAND WEIGHT
HORSE SHOE
FROG
ACORN
CANDLE
WORM
TEPEE
SHOE
MAIL BAG
RULER
RABBIT
LOAF OF BREAD

I'm my mom's kid!
HOME SWEET HOME
#1 MOM
MOM
MOM
HAPPY MOTHER'S DAY!
M is for Mom!
Hi Mom
To: MOM
Are you your kid's mom?
BASEBALL BAT
BRUSH
BOOT
HOE
BIRD
POCKET KNIFE
CHALK ERASER
BOWL
UMBRELLA
RULER
TELESCOPE
LADDER
SPOOL of THREAD
(4) HEARTS
(3) TEPEES
BOOTIE
FRYING PAN
CANOE
SHELL
CROWN
MUSHROOM

GET WELL SOON!
GET WELL QUICK
201
I want to be a Nurse.
Patient
Sick Dog
© Liz Ball
Am I a Flu bug?
FLAG
CHERRY
(3) SOCKS
SHOE
BALL
ENVELOPE
PIPE
NEEDLE
STICK OF GUM
PEAR
CANDY CORN
BOWL
CROSS
PENCIL
COIN
(2) BIRDS
SYRINGE
RULER
CANDLE
TEPEE

POISON IVY HAS 3 LEAVES.
Names of POISONOUS PLANTS
SLIPPERY ELM
SASSAFRAS
WILD FLOWERS
NATURE TRAIL
TREES
DOGWOOD
LIVERLEAF
VIOLETS
FOXGLOVE
BLOODROOT
SMARTWEED
HERB ROBERT
RATTLESNAKE ROOT
I am a Naturalist
SOCK
GRASSHOPPER
NEEDLE
SHARK
CROWN
BRUSH
ELEPHANT HEAD
FISHHOOK
BELL
CAMP KNIFE
CLOTHES-PIN
(3) BIRDS
SLIPPER
BABY BOOTIE
BOOT
DOG HEAD
(2) FISH
IRON
SHOVEL
TEPEE
RULER
PEAR
SPOON
TOOTHBRUSH
PENCIL
PINE TREE
CARROT

Did you ever lose a contact lens?
CAN YOU SEE THIS?
Are you an Optometrist?
PENCIL
PAINTBRUSH
CANOE
BALLOON
FISH HOOK
DOG
CARDINAL
MOUSE
HAT
LIGHT BULB
MUSHROOM
BIRD
ICE CREAM BAR
SOCK
CROSS
WHALE
SHOE
BRUSH
CANDY CANE
COMB
CONE

CONGRATULATIONS!
Your braces are coming off today!
T. Alligator
P. Panda
L. Ball
S. Bear
New Patients
Rabbit
Rat
Mous
A-J
Q-
K-P
V-Z
Adults have braces, too.
Do Orthodontists like teeth?
I have braces!
SMILE
©Liz Ball
(2) LADDERS
(2) TUBES OF TOOTHPASTE
(4) TOOTH BRUSHES
(3) ELASTICS
RETAINER
(2) PENCILS
TEPEE
THERMOS
SCALER
CROWN
MIRROR
ENVELOPE
CRAYON
IRON
CUP
HEART
MIRROR
GUM
TULIP
PEAR
(2) SOCKS

Alpha Bravo Charlie Delta Echo Foxtrot Golf Hotel India Juliette Kilo Lima Mike November
I like to fly.
What is your favorite plane?
My son is a pilot!
© Liz Ball
UMBRELLA
BOWL
FUNNEL
(2) HEARTS
LIPS
(2) CUPCAKES
CHICKEN
COMB
BOOMERANG
MUSHROOM
MOUSE HEAD
LIGHTBULB
PANTS
BANANA
(2) CONES
(2) CROWNS
ICE SKATE
CARROT
Oscar Papa Quebec Romeo Sierra Tango Uniform Victor Whiskey X-ray Yankee Zulu

Dial 911 in an Emergency
The Rovers
ROVER
K-9
TRACKER
POLICE
K-9
Liz Ball '98
Are you a Policeman?
P
2 CANOES
ALLIGATOR
CUP
SOCK
RULER
WRISTWATCH
SNOW SHOVEL
(2) CONES
LOLLIPOP
MITTEN
ROOSTER
NEEDLE
ACORN
CARROT
WORM
SNAKE
MUSIC NOTE
MUSHROOM
SODA

Do you have a pet?
©Liz Ball
I work in a Pet store.
Flea
CROWN
(2) PENCILS
CANOE
UNICORN
SLICE of CAKE
MUG
KNIFE
(2) BIRDS
TEPEE
LADY BUG
HARE
HORSE
SALT-SHAKER
ACORN
SHOE
HEART
DOLPHIN
SNAKE
BOWL
LADDER

Jo likes to make quilts.
Are you a Quilter?
© Liz Ball 2001
PIZZA SLICE
ENVELOPE
QUARTER
CONE
IRON
CHEESE SLICER
LADDER
CUP
FLYSWATTER
GEM
BIRDHOUSE
PIN WHEEL
DOMINO
QUEEN
QUART JAR
QUAIL
SAILBOAT
SHOE
KNIFE
CHERRY
CHEESE
(2) TEPEES
CROWN
BELL
BALL
CANDLE

GO
OLYMPIC
GAMES
GO!
R
33
5
101
59
23
311
2
©Lin Ball
I am a Runner
PANTS
CANOE
SLICE OF BREAD
(3) SOCKS
(3) ICE CREAM CONES
WATCH
SNAKE
WORM
(2) CARROTS
(2) CUPS
MATCH
CANDLE
MUSIC NOTE
HEART
PEAR
MUSHROOM
TOOTHBRUSH
LOLLIPOP
BANANA

SPECIAL
2ND PAIR
1/2 PRICE!
SIZE 13
SIZE 10
SIZE 11
SIZE 8
SIZE 12
SIZE 12
HOPPER HEELS
TOAD LOAFERS
XL
S
M
M
XXL
Yikes! What a lot of shoes!
Are you a shoe Salesman?
Is her name Imelda?
©Liz Ball
MUG
(2) CONES
BOOK
ENVELOPE
IRON
RULER
STICK OF GUM
FLAG
HEART
SALT SHAKER
BIRD
TROWEL
CANDLE
SPOON
DOG
CROWN
TEPEE
STOCKING
MOUSE
CROWN
CHICK

I am a Soprano.
I sing alto.
I am a Singer.
BAAABER SHOP QUARTET
©Liz Ball
SNAKE
ELF HAT
HIGH HEEL SHOE
(2) MUSIC NOTES
CHICK
SKILLET
NEEDLE
SOCK
BADMINTON BIRDY
LEMON
(2) SHOES
JAR
WORM
BELL
SPOON
CANDLE
(2) KNIVES
BIRD
(3) HEARTS
CHOPSTICKS

SWINE SCHOOL IS FUN!
OINK
LUNCH
LUNCH
©Liz Ball
I am a Student!
BALL BAT
(3) HEARTS
RULER
BIRD
AXE
(2) PENCILS
SOCK
ENVELOPE
TEPEE
MUSHROOM
(2) CANDLES
CANOE
STICK OF GUM
BOOT
PEAR
PIE
FLAG
CROSS
BOW
CUPCAKE
CRAYON

Will you be a Teacher?
COUNT BY 2's
2 4 6 8 10
12 14 16 18 20
22 24 26 28 30
32 34 36 38 40
42 44 46 48 50
EVEN NUMBERS
2 4 6 8 10
MATH BOOKS
©Liz Ball
(4) PENCILS
(2) BATS
(2) RULERS
(2) BIRDS
(2) SOCKS
(2) PIE SLICES
(2) TOOTHBRUSHES
(2) CANOES
(2) FLAGS
(2) CRUTCHES
(2) HEARTS

JIM'S TOW
JT
JIM'S TOW
Do you need a tow?
I drive a Tow Truck.
BRUSH
HORSESHOE
PENCIL
TEACUP
LIGHTBULB
ACORN
SLICE OF BREAD
HAMMER
KNIFE
CROSS
PAINT BRUSH
NEEDLE
POPSICLE
SPOON
STOCKING
BOWL
SNOW SHOVEL
CARROT
LADDER
BOOK
RULER
CANOE
SPIDER
MATCH

No.
9
LIZ
I like Trains!
LADDER
MITTEN
ORANGE SLICE
PITCHER
SPOOL OF THREAD
WRENCH
HIGH HEEL
PIE SLICE
FROG
ICE CREAM CONE
PENCIL
SPOON
PAINT BRUSH
CROWN
CARROT
RABBIT
SAILBOAT
CUP
TULIP
TOOTH BRUSH

Are you a Trash collector?
Do you recycle?
FLAG
CHICK
CARROT
ORANGE SLICE
BREAD
BAT
OWL
CROWN
YAM
(2) TEPEES
HARE
(2) HEARTS
JAR
BEET
BOW
BLUEJAY
KNIFE
PIE
(2) SHOES
PENCIL
ONION
POP
©Liz Ball

Wow! Those mice can sew!
Liz Ball
Tailors sew clothes.
DRUMSTICK
FLUTE
FISH
WORM
BOOTIE
POPSICLE
LIGHTBULB
(2) BRUSHES
PIE
BOAT
(2) HATS
GOLF CLUB
CANOE
LADDER
SHOE
THIMBLE

UPTOWN SCOREBOARD
HOME
U
AWAY
2
1
UMP
CANINE CLEANERS
DOGGY CHEWS ARE UNIQUE!
UPTOWN UNIFORMS
BOW WOW SODA
U TEAM
Is the ump always right?
Do you have a favorite team?
I am an Umpire.
© Liz Ball
SHOE
JAR
CROWN
GUM
(2) PENCILS
BATON
BOOMERANG
UMBRELLA
TURTLE
TEPEE
CONE
SAILBOAT
COIN
NEEDLE
MUG
SOCK
CUPCAKE
TOOTHBRUSH
HEART

The Unicorn is washing my underwear.
CUP
STETHOSCOPE
(2) UMBRELLAS
KITCHEN UTENSIL
BIRD
CANDLE
TIARA
(2) SPOONS
BALL
HOUSE
EYE GLASSES
SALT SHAKER
BAND-AID
LADY BUG
(2) HEARTS
MOTH
PENNY
BUTTON
BELL
FLASHLIGHT
CAKE

ICE
BONE SODA
PUPPY TAN
MUTT SPF 15
We're on Vacation.
HEART
MATCH
RABBIT
BOWLING PIN
BALL BAT
WORM
TULIP
BOWL
NAIL
ICE CREAM CONE
SPIDER
SALT SHAKER
ELF HAT
BASEBALL
CARROT
FISH HOOK
ENVELOP
HOUSE
MOUSE
TEPEE
V

Can you play the Violin?
©Liz Ball
Hi
CATERPILLAR
(2) BUTTERFLIES
KNIFE
BEETLE
EARTH WORM
BANANA
COIN
BIRD
SHOE
TURNIP
(2) RULERS
(2) SPOONS
(4) MUSIC NOTES
SOCK
VALENTINE
HORSE

MENU
HAMBURGERS
HOT DOGS
FRIES
TACOS
ICE CREAM
SODA
FLOATS
SUNDAES
MENU
I'll order a watermelon milkshake
I'm a Waitress
© Liz Ball
PIE
CUPCAKE
PARSNIP
ICE CREAM CONE
SOCK
(2) HEARTS
BRUSH
PEAR
CAKE
LOLLIPOP
(2) STICKS OF GUM
BONE
FISH
RING
BOWL
(3) CUPS
W

Wow! I can be a TV Weatherman.
BEARLY NEWS
WEATHER
RAIN
BEAR WEEK
RAINY DAY TALES
H
L
Do you think it will rain today?
NEEDLE
HAT
LADDER
LIGHT-BULB
CUP
EYE GLASSES
HEART
Flicker
LIGHTNING
WOODPECKER
CHERRY
THERMOMETER
TOOTH-BRUSH
ENVELOPE
MUSHROOM
BOOT
MITTEN
SUN
CANOE
TEPEE
CROSS
SHELL

I'm a whittler
GLUE
VARNISH
CARVE
WHITTLE
LORIS
CHIP CARVING
© Liz Ball
FLASHLIGHT
FISH HOOK
BAND-AID
STICK OF BUTTER
(2) ENVELOPES
BRUSH
(3) CARVING KNIVES
SOCK
SCREW
SOAP
CRAYON
FLOWER POT
(2) TEPEES
PENNY
GUM
PENNANT
MALLET
HEART
RULER
(2) FLAGS

FIREWOOD FOR SALE
Are you a Woodcutter?
WOW! what a chain!
© Liz Ball
CROWN
BOW
BAT
NAIL
TOOTHBRUSH
BIRD
OIL LAMP
SCREW
ART BRUSH
BOOT
EYE GLASSES
SOCK
ALLIGATOR
LIGHT BULB
(2) HEARTS
ARROWHEAD
CONE
CANDY CORN
DONUT
PIE
LEMON
CANDLE
BONE
TEPEE
MATCH
NEEDLE
CHAIN SAW
MALLET

Grizzly
X - Ray
Technician
Do X-ray Technicians take pictures?
X is for X-ray.
©Liz Ball
PICTURE FRAME
CANOE
SOCK
TOOTHBRUSH
BOOMERANG
ENVELOPE
PENCIL
PARTY HAT
THERMOMETER
FRIED EGG
MUSHROOM
FLUTE
SOAP
CANDY STICK
EGG
BOLT
STICK OF GUM
TEPEE
PENNY
HEART
STETHOSCOPE
PLIERS
SHOE
X

Can you "Walk the Dog" or do "Cat in the Cradle"?
YOYO CHAMP
©Liz Ball
I like to Yoyo!
CARROT
HEART
THIMBLE
BIRD
(3) CONES
JAR
LADDER
(9) BANANAS
SHOE
BALL
MUSHROOM
CANDY CORN
TURTLE
FLAG
RULER
BRUSH

Did you find all the hidden objects?
I want to be a Zookeeper!
©Liz Ball
Adios
What is your favorite job?
Bye!
A-Z
ARROWHEAD
EGG
ICE CREAM CONE
JAR
KITE
NOTE
QUARTER
ROBIN
UNICORN
XYLOPHONE
BONE
FLUTE
VALENTINE
YOYO
CARROT
GONDOLA
SPOON
OLIVE
DAGGER
HAMMER
LIGHT BULB
MUG
PEAR
TURTLE
WHALE
ZIRCONIUM DIAMOND